THE ADVENTURES OF STEAMO THE WONDER CRAB

THE ADVENTURES OF STEAMO THE WONDER CRAB

By Michael Miller, M.Ed., M.S.

Illustrations by Jeffrey Vernon

PYRAMID PRESS

Copyright © 2016 Michael Miller, M.Ed., M.S.

All rights reserved. No part of this book, in part or in whole, may be reproduced, transmitted, or utilized, in any form or by any means, electronic or mechanical, including photocopying, recording, or by any information storage and retrieval system, without permission in writing from the publisher, except for brief quotations in critical articles, books and reviews.

International Standard Book Number-10: 0-9899017-9-3
International Standard Book Number-13: 978-0-9899017-9-6

First Pyramid Press Edition 2016

The paper used in this publication meets the minimum requirements of the American National Standard for Permanence of Paper for Printed Library Materials Z39.48-1984

PYRAMID PRESS
9550 South Eastern Avenue • Suite 253
Las Vegas, NV 89123 U.S.A.
contact@pyramidpress.net

Acknowledgments

The author wants to happily acknowledge and greedily thank the following awesome people without whom this unusual book would have likely remained just an interesting idea:

Bruce Herman, Minhee Choe,
Dr. Liz, Ed Dornberger, Chuck Parcell,
David Rice, James Moushoul,
Johnny Cochran, and Carl Evans.

All these wonderful people played different and important roles in motivating and expanding on ideas for the author. Without this motivation and these ideas Steamo wouldn't be the amazing wonder crab he turned out to be.

A profound and heartfelt thank you is expressed to all and to the readers of this book.

Introduction

The story of Steamo the Wonder Crab is an amazing and true story beginning in the waters of Fukushima, Japan in 2011.

Steamo was not always a wonder crab. Once he was a normal crab living a normal crab life around the nuclear power plant at Fukushima. Neither the earthquake or the tsunami that followed it on March 11, 2011 killed Steamo. While the Fukushima disaster produced the largest discharge of radioactive material into the ocean in history, and it was this radiation that changed Steamo into the Magical wonder crab that he is today.

Steamo was transformed into a 9' tall neon pink magical crab. Steamo quickly learned he could fly and change his size at will. If needed Steamo could shrink to the size of a dime, and just as easily change back to being 9' tall.

After the disaster Steamo had come to learn the entire crab population around Fukushima was wiped out, along with many other species in his habitat. Prudently Steamo decided to relocate and embarked on a great adventure to see the rest of the world.

Steamo started off on a random journey through the ocean. His first encounter was with a friendly group of American sailors in the middle of the sea. He found them interesting and with their encouragement decided to set a course for America, specifically southern California.

While in no rush, Steamo made his journey to America through the Gulf of Mexico. It was a leisurely trip. While there Steamo made the acquaintance of Soberanis, a 1950s robot cast adrift in the ocean rusting away. Steamo took Soberanis to land and set about the task of drying him out. Steamo had his first friend and Soberanis had a new life. They became inseparable and journeyed together to America.

Steamo explained to Soberanis the purpose of his journey to America. He was like a modern day Columbus, setting out to explore and discover a new land and new people.

Because water, especially ocean water is not good for robots, Steamo flew Soberanis to America and landed in Hollywood. Not knowing the area at all, Steamo landed randomly at Vermont and Franklin in the House of Pies parking lot. This was the starting point of their adventures and their discovery of America.

Naturally, the site of a 9' tall, neon pink, talking crab who could fly was pretty shocking to most people who came in contact with him. It so happens, Hollywood has quite a few oddities of it's own so Steamo wasn't a total outcast.

Steamo and Soberanis set out to explore Hollywood and the surrounding areas in earnest. Their mission was to observe people and create interactions that would be informative and instructive to humans. The stories, lessons and anecdotal insights that follow are a direct result of Steamo's adventures. While Steamo became a legendary character and Hollywood icon to many, Soberanis stayed in the background and was a mystery. If one can image the odd site of a 9' tall neon pink magical talking crab, the site of his pal Soberanis was even more unusual. Soberanis was stuck in a time warp of sorts. He was quintessential 1950s and about 5' tall. He made odd clicking sounds and feed back noises constantly.

It was these noises that attracted one particular "stray dog", a transient who was called Enema Greg (E.G.). E.G. was an idiot savant who was making his home in Griffith Park, in the northern part of the Hollywood Hills. E.G. came into the city a few times a week to panhandle and gather food. As he travelled on foot, he too would make odd sounds and clicking noises. Although unclear who heard the others' noises first, Soberanis and E.G. were on a sonar collision course.

E.G. was a friendly sort, originally from the Midwest. He couldn't hold a job due to his instability and frequent need to self medicate. He had a friendly and disarming personality and he was quirky, but he had the ability to hide this from most people. If he was around you long enough his constant lying patterns became obvious. E.G. was self taught and well read. He actually was a genius and had an uncanny ability to explain the most complex things in a simple way. As a younger man he had spent several years interacting with a great guru through email. This helped shape him and caused him to withdraw from his family and question his Catholic upbringing.

After being fired from yet another job, E.G. travelled to Hollywood for a fresh start and with an idea to join Scientology. This was unsuccessful, as the Scientologists would have nothing to do with this homeless genius, who looked like a hobo. After E.G. was no longer able to take advantage of his only friend in Hollywood, he became homeless and found refuge and acceptance from Steamo. E.G. enjoyed his freedom immensely, yet this didn't stop him from spending days at a time following Steamo around. In fact, Steamo became his new guru and Soberanis became his friend.

Nurse Barb wasn't really a nurse at all, she was a crazed blonde former bombshell who met E.G. at Palermo's Italian restaurant. Palermo's was a Hollywood institution primarily known for giving any policeman on duty $5.00 dinners. On any given day, at any given time the restaurant was filled with free-loading cops taking advantage of this perk. Police from every jurisdiction within 50 miles were found inside the friendly confines of Palermo's eating for almost nothing.

It happened one day that Nurse Barb was in Hollywood and stopped in at Palermo's. She was friendly with the pizza delivery man, a 55 year old loser who went by the name Bob. Bob had horrible body odor and was a loud glad handler and sycophant. This fat sociopath delivered pizza, but told the customers and his friends he was the manager of the restaurant.

Bob wasn't all bad, like most sociopaths he could be charming and endearing as well as a fantastic and entertaining liar. This common ground is what led to E.G. endearing himself to Bob, and led to free food at least twice a week. In one of life's odd synchronicities, there was one occasion when E.G. was picking up his free food while Nurse Barb wandered in to see Bob. Although it started with a friendly introduction, it didn't take long for E.G. to engage Nurse Barb in mental games. This led to a relationship of sorts, as Nurse Barb thought E.G. was normal and a potential sex friend.

Nurse Barb was much older than E.G., easily mid to late 50s. She was a buxom woman, blonde and lonely. Nurse Barb knew Bob because Bob's mother was her neighbor and often served as her caretaker to earn extra money. She was both friendly and depressed, often giddy and quite insane. E.G. was a quick read of people and figured out Nurse Barb pretty fast. E.G. liked to have fun at her expense and readily knew what buttons to push and how to get the Nurse to have temper fits. It was in this spirit he decided to introduce her to Steamo one day.

Nurse Barb lived in a 55 and older trailer park in Palm Springs. She claimed to have retired at age 40 as a bank President, although she couldn't do basic math and had no college degree. She was both needy and clingy and at the same time bossy. She needed to be needed and was highly sexualized. She had the sexual appetite of a 20 year old USC sorority girl. She was so driven by her insatiable sexual desires, E.G. first lured her to meet Steamo with the promise of sexual favors from a 9' tall magical crab.

Nurse Barb and Enema Greg became regular followers of Steamo. They loved the validation they got from being in his company. While they both knew Steamo was an intellectual giant and their teacher and guru, it was much harder for Nurse Barb to learn from him. It wasn't just that she was of average intelligence, it was more how emotional she would get. Her frequent emotional meltdowns got in her way of learning and even hearing Steamo's wisdom. E.G. partially hung around Steamo because Nurse Barb was a fun and easy target to torment. It was like picking low hanging fruit.

As Steamo and his odd group of friends explore Hollywood and America, they meet new people, encounter odd situations and have fun. This is done as Steamo learns about Americans and dispenses great wisdom and knowledge to those he comes into contact with, as well as the followers of his adventures.

Steamo hopes you enjoy his adventures and are able to learn from his wisdom, just as Enema Greg and Nurse Barb have. Who knew one could benefit so much from the teachings of a 9' tall neon pink talking magical crab?

Table of Contents

Introduction   vii

Chapter 1   **Who Is Steamo?**   1

Chapter 2   **Steamo's Interesting Observations**   33

Chapter 3   **Steamo's Experiences with Love and Friendship**   71

Chapter 4   **Steamo's Guide to Success**   85

Chapter 5   **Steamo's Opinions about Religion**   115

Chapter 6   **Steamo's Wisdom about Vice**   119

Chapter 7   **Steamo's Ideas about Sex**   135

Chapter 8   **Steamo's Advice on Peacefulness**   145

Chapter 1
Who Is Steamo?

When Steamo was a small crab he was told, "Be yourself. An original is always worth more than a copy."

Steamo sees the invisible, feels the intangible and achieves the impossible.

If forced to pick his favorite English word Steamo would say "Wow!" It is a small and easy word, great to text and encapsulates many things. Nothing is better than a word that is short and to the point thought Steamo.

Although Steamo can fly, he sometimes prefers to walk to where he must go. This provides him with exercise, and it prevents him from becoming too isolated from society that he becomes afraid of it.

Steamo creates his own culture.

Steamo likes to hunt his own meat. He has the tools, the instincts and the will to do this effectively. The hunt becomes a meditation for him… it is primal and immediate. Unlike many other things in the human world which he chooses to dwell in, at present. He eats everything he kills. If he cannot eat it all himself, he leaves some for the scavengers. Even maggots have to eat.

Steamo made a toast at a wedding he attended. He raised his glass and looked at the groom's father and said, "Here's to you, you're true blue. Men like you are few. You're really above the class. Yes you are, you horse's ass!"

Once Steamo told his pal that a person's qualities are not determined by their race. He said, "They are determined by their actions." His friend asked, "Does that mean there are no differences between races?" Steamo replied, "You are talking to a sentient magical crab! My race is quite different from yours in many ways. However, my actions determine my being."

Steamo could have a mild case of Tourette's—one day he blurted out "Hi hot and a hell of a lot!"

Steamo possesses a rare gift, he brings confidence to those around him without being arrogant!

Steamo is like a river. He touches things lightly or deeply and moves along, as life moves along.

Steamo is quick to listen and slow to speak.

Once an old man told Steamo a limerick he liked very much. It went like this: "Fire, fire, false alarm. Baby shit on father's arm. Father went to get a switch, and baby called him a son of a bitch." Steamo repeated this many times. He liked the sound of it.

Steamo believes that those speaking Glossolalia come closest to speaking the native language of Magical Crabs.

Steamo is an omnivore, and can survive by eating many different kinds of food. If he is able to, he likes to eat a wide variety of foods, from a variety of different sources. In this way, he provides his body with a broad spectrum of nutrients that he might otherwise miss out on.

Steamo said, "I like to defend those that cannot defend themselves, if they are worthy." He was asked, "How do you know if they are worthy?" He replied, "They are worthy if I deem them to be so...I am strong, so it is my right. Whoever disagrees with my judgement can test their strength against mine."

Steamo drove by a building while driving his custom Porsche. The sign said, "Life is about Love and Truth. It is not about Ego." Steamo tore down the sign as he hates meaningless phrases.

Steamo is a crab of action, not of words.

Steamo doesn't read Nietzsche, Marx or Hitler.

Steamo can be a rebel. Steamo can be a cad. If any player haters run into Steamo, he clips off both their nads.

Steamo has a black belt in SARCASM. He can take you down with one remark.

Steamo heard a phrase once from one of his friends in the Army. He liked it and used it himself. The phrase was "Fuck, fight, or hold the light."

Like all crabs, Steamo sometimes likes to eat feces. He is not embarrassed about this, for the simple reason that he does not care what some humans might think about him. He is who he is.

Steamo heals and hurts and does both as needed and required.

"Amazing," thought Steamo one day, "how much time the average human being spends talking every day. It seems at times as if they fear silence."

Sometimes Steamo is like a parrot. He can't help imitating sounds that he hears.

    Steamo was walking down the street. A bum asked him if he had a quarter. Steamo said, "Yes" and continued walking. Further down the street he saw a homeless woman. She was huddled next to a building, asleep. Steamo walked on. Toward the end of his walk a young man approached him and asked him if he could please spare a little change so he could get a bus ticket. Steamo gave him a dollar.

Steamo likes limericks. One of his favorites is "I am frightened, you are frightened. It is time to get our trousers tightened."

Steamo is a poet. Naughty little poems make him feel better. An example of such a little ditty is: *Milk, milk, lemonade, around the corner, fudge is made.*

Steamo thinks any man who doesn't follow his emotions is a foolish man.

Steamo gives to man much more than man gives to him. He likes it that way.

Steamo says animals are not lawn ornaments! If humans are not going to let them live in their home and make them part of their family, they should re-home them.

Chapter 2
Steamo's Interesting Observations

Steamo has observed that many humans must be taught on the same level as a dog in order to get them to alter their behavior in the slightest.

Steamo has learned there is another intelligence in the human body. It is the GUT.

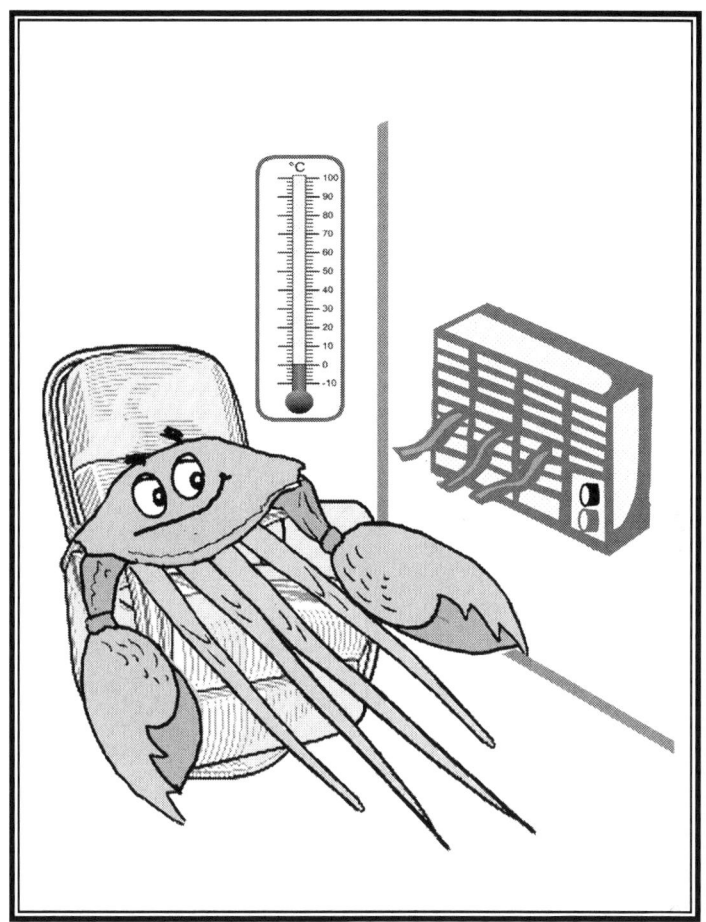

Steamo likes many things about being in the human world. The comfort of air conditioning is one such thing. Steamo considers this a wonderful invention.

Steamo observed many humans push the elevator button many times. He wonders if doing so more than once makes it arrive faster?

Sharing a meal with a human is the second most intimate thing you can do with a person.

Steamo wonders if illiterate humans get the full effect of Alphabet Soup.

Steamo heard 90% of the world doesn't really care about your problems, and the other 10% are glad you have them. This really got Steamo thinking.

Steamo noted a man dangling from a cliff will reach out his hand to his worst enemy.

Steamo told someone that even shit is sometimes useful.

Steamo thinks feelings are not real. He observed them to be conditioned chemical responses.

Steamo noted all humans could take a lesson from the weather. It pays no attention to criticism.

While in the human world Steamo learned that aggression can be a sign of weakness.

At times, Steamo thinks that words can be like a monkey holding a loaded gun to it's own head.

A know-it-all radio show host accused Steamo of being mean. Steamo retorted, "There is a difference between being mean and being accurate."

Steamo noticed that everybody wants to come to the party...but no one wants to help set up.

A shallow blonde reporter, from Channel 5 News, caught up with Steamo once, after he made an appearance at a charity event. He was asked who were some humans that he admired. The answer was Groucho Marx, Ronald Reagan, Albert Einstein and Vlad Tepish. Steamo appreciated that each used the normal in a novel way.

Steamo has noticed truth in prejudices.

Steamo has learned the greater a person's sense of guilt, the greater their need to blame others.

Steamo observed a lot about humans by the way they handle these three things—a rainy day, lost luggage and tangled Christmas tree lights.

Steamo encountered a young couple. They wore shabby clothing and their hair was long and unkept, but not naturally so…it looked like they worked to make it look that way. They told him that he must save the planet. Steamo asked them if they thought the planet was alive. They said, "Yes." Steamo asked them, "What does evolution teach us about an organism that cannot save itself?"

Steamo observed the only difference between a rut and a grave is the depth.

Steamo believes you can feed anyone a fifty pound turkey, as long as it's one bite at a time.

Steamo figured out if you hold a person under water long enough, they stop being an asshole.

Steamo told Nurse Barb, who was 56, living in a 55 and over trailer park, "In the land of the blind, the one eyed man is king."

Steamo asked a priest this question after a baptism, "If corn oil is made from corn and vegetable oil is made from vegetables, then what is baby oil made from?"

Steamo told his good pal, The Evil Plumber, "Water finds its own level."

Steamo wonders who was the first human to look at a cow and think, "I'll squeeze these dangly things and drink whatever comes out."

When asked what animal he admired, Steamo answered, "The octopus. It is highly intelligent. It is highly adaptable. It understands the art of camouflage, and hiding in plain site. It is an efficient and remarkable hunter. It is beautiful."

A young man who was taken advantage of in a purchase complained to Steamo about his misfortune. Steamo counseled the youngster "The bad purchase was not a misfortune at all, rather, it was tuition."

Steamo finds humans who think they know everything to be boring.

Steamo met a psychotic nurse named Barb, who lived to place blame on people. Blame placing is a fool's game and a weak tool to cover for guilt.

Steamo was soaring through the air when a guided missile struck him. He crashed to the ground, dazed and slightly injured. He realized he had flown too close to a government zone and had set off their radar. Instead of taking the attack personally, and destroying the place, he made a note to self "avoid if possible next time."

Steamo has observed that some women are like the Vietcong—they use make-up like camouflage.

The quality of our enemies does us honor... or dishonor.

Steamo believes documentary film makers are devious.

Steamo thinks that people in power who destroy rather than create need to be exterminated.

The more time Steamo spends around humans, the more Steamo likes pitbulls.

All living things seek to protect themselves. When the snake bites it is not personal—you stepped on it's tail, that's all.

Chapter 3
Steamo's Experiences with Love and Friendship

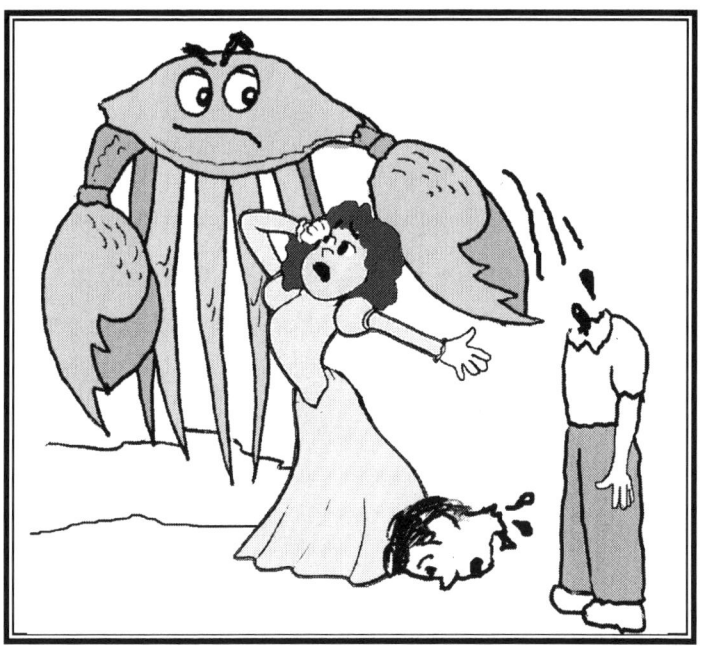

Steamo advises human friends, just because someone is a DRAMA QUEEN doesn't mean you have to treat them like royalty!

Steamo believes hugging is good medicine. It transfers energy and gives the hugged person an emotional lift. Hugging is a form of communication, it can say things you don't have words for.

Steamo noticed that humans, both wise and foolish, frequently think love and permission are the same.

Steamo believes that dogs are the only thing in the world that will love you more than they love themselves.

Steamo is often friendly. But that doesn't mean he's a friend.

Steamo makes it a habit to compliment three people every day.

Confidence is the ability to feel beautiful without needing someone to tell you first, but smiling when someone does.

Because life can be tough for many people Steamo makes the effort to be friendly when he sees humans. It doesn't cost extra to be nice and it may help someone have a better day.

Some people prefer to use language to heal and inspire. Others prefer to use words to injure and destroy. Steamo does not prefer either one; he uses whichever serves his purpose at the time.

Steamo was invited to dinner by a woman and her husband, who he had helped in some small way. He refused politely at first, but upon their insistence, he relented. At dinner, they were very uncomfortable, as they wanted to please him, but frankly did not know what he liked to eat. He noticed the tension and said, "Thank you for this food. I like to eat many different things, but it is the company of a meal that I enjoy most."

One of Steamo's most intelligent friends often appears to be quite insane. It was then that Steamo learned that there is a very fine line between insanity and genius.

Steamo remarked to one of his friends, "Here's to those who wish us well, those that don't can go to hell."

Steamo and his friends don't pay too much heed to labels. What sheep and insects think isn't important to Steamo.

Steamo keeps it R.E.A.L.
He *Remembers Everybody Ain't Loyal.*

Chapter 4
Steamo's Guide to Success

On the road to success, Steamo advises to remember never to confuse activity with achievement!

Steamo points out: "Life isn't a straight road. There is a curve called failure. A loop called confusion. Speed bumps called friends. Red lights called enemies. Caution signs called family. And sometimes you have flat tires called jobs. But if you have a spare called determination, and the engine called perseverance, you'll make it to a place called SUCCESS!"

Steamo likes using America's favorite breakfast plate of bacon and eggs to explain the difference between "dedication" and "commitment"–The chicken is dedicated whereas the pig is committed.

While Steamo's wisdom is well known, it is clear that many receive his advice but only the wise profit from it.

Steamo had a friend, a man of quality. Steamo shared the observation with him, "Fantasy is fine, and can be useful, but only insofar as it teaches us something about reality. If you can learn to live and operate more in reality, than in fantasy, you will have an advantage over the great majority of human beings alive today."

Steamo thinks being happy is a decision. People can be as happy as they want to be, if they so choose.

Steamo observed assertive people can come across as more intelligent than those who are more reserved.

Steamo has been asked over and over again what are the most important qualities one should possess in approaching a daunting task. Other than intelligence and emotional stability the two most important qualities are *Persistence* and *Determination*. Steamo often tells people the secret of his success adapting to the human world: "I Will Persist Until I Succeed."

Listening is an important skill thought Steamo. Yet, most humans listen with the intent to reply, not the intent to understand.

Steamo secretly told an old friend that loser humans make excuses while the winner humans get to sleep with the prom queen.

Steamo doesn't chase money. Steamo lets money chase him.

Steamo advised a young man who was pondering whether to attempt a rigorous task: "Decide if you want it more than you're afraid of it."

Steamo realized long ago there is no such thing as staying the same. If you are not gaining ground, you are losing ground.

Whatever Steamo's mind can conceive and believe—it will achieve.

Steamo's friendly reminder to humans—your life is unwritten, so write a best seller.

Steamo likes to acquire money. It allows a man or a crab to express his will on society.

Steamo owns a well made bow. He is an excellent archer known for great accuracy. Despite that, Steamo must have a target to shoot at or he will be wasting his great efforts.

Steamo sees tragedy as an opportunity.

Steamo lives by the motto—anything worth doing, is worth doing right.

Steamo believes a lifestyle is something you pay for, while a life is what pays for you.

An old man told Steamo, "Money isn't worth anything unless you spend it." He was broke.

Steamo once told a younger friend, "Live life looking through the windshield, not through the rearview mirror." Steamo knows one can't start the next chapter of life if one keeps re-reading the last one.

Steamo respects men of action. As a small crab Steamo learned "idea men" are a dime a dozen.

Steamo advises Enema Greg and Nurse Barb, "Every morning you have two choices, continue to sleep with your dreams or wake up and chase them."

Steamo's NO EXCUSE RULE: "Make yourself stronger than your excuses!"

Empty pockets never held anyone back! Only empty heads and hearts can do that. "What's your excuse?" Steamo asked Enema Greg.

If you are moving slow, Steamo reminds you that slow motion is better than no motion.

The best advice Steamo shared is "Find something you love and let it kill you."

Challenges are what make life interesting, and overcoming them is what makes life meaningful.

Steamo is obsessed with simplicity. And making things SIMPLE is very, very HARD.

Chapter 5
Steamo's Ideas about Religion

Steamo notes the majority is the safe place to be for most humans.

Steamo is a regular attendee at various religious services. In doing so Steamo has learned an important truism: for true believers no proof is necessary while for non-believers no proof is sufficient.

Steamo has observed good men in bad churches and bad men in good ones.

Deceitful humans get Steamo angry, thus he considers most priests and policemen as true enemies.

Chapter 6
Steamo's Wisdom about Vices

People push you to your limits, but when you finally explode and fight back—you're the mean one!

Steamo doesn't favor fortune tellers. He believes the best way to predict the future is to create it.

Steamo told Nurse Barb, "Whatever the problem is, the answer is not in the fridge!"

Steamo met a shyster lawyer, then Steamo realized one lawyer with a briefcase can steal more than 100 men with guns.

Steamo never interrupts an enemy while they are making a mistake.

Steamo met an old man that told him how to tell when a politician is lying—when his lips are moving! Steamo doesn't believe liberals—they use words to hide their true intentions.

Although Steamo has the power and cunning to easily take what he wants, he prefers to trade for it instead. This keeps people friendly, and makes things easier on him. Steamo says one should never steal what can be given in exchange for something you have. And never steal what can be given freely if you ask.

After spending a short time in America Steamo concluded the U.S. prison system is just another form of slavery.

It occurred to Steamo, that what is deemed criminal in one environment can be deemed virtuous in another. The opposite is also true. Steamo wondered if there is anything inherently good or bad in any action...except what others judge them to possess.

After meeting a big blonde woman in a power suit, who was a junior college president, lusting for power, Steamo called the woman "a black hearted bitch whose heart pumps piss."

Once Steamo attended Santa Anita Race Track on opening day. When asked for his thoughts on the experience, he quipped, "There are certainly more horses' asses here than there are horses."

Steamo detests liars, and Steamo counts half truths as lies. Humans seem to lie for two reasons observed Steamo. They want to make themselves look better or to protect themselves.

Steamo noticed that in big cities police are like sophisticated predators...often hiding and ready to pounce on unsuspecting prey.

Steamo learned that vodka is like a crab. It crawls right on top of you.

Unlike humans, Steamo has learned to avoid self-destructive moments and habits.

Steamo met a lady who was a college president in Chicago. He noted that she had risen rapidly in the ranks due to her sexual prowess and appetite. Steamo told Soberanis if she had as many pricks coming out of her as going in to her, she would be a porcupine.

Chapter 7
Steamo's Ideas about Sex

Steamo became physically involved with a female crab. She made increasing demands on his time and resources. Then Steamo realized many think a kiss is a contract and a hug a commitment.

Steamo went to a massage parlour and got undressed. A Korean lady came into the room, pointed at Steamo's largest claw and asked, "Okay to touch?"

Steamo pointed out to a prostitute "for every minute one is angry one loses sixty seconds of happiness."

Steamo once crossed a friend's wife. It was then that Steamo learned that 'Who Who Ha Ha' is undefeated.

Steamo became entangled with a crazed nurse who became addicted to his magical crab urine. Steamo's warm and yellow became her pleasure tonic. It seemed to give her comfort.

Steamo had a young male friend, who liked to brag about all the women he had slept with. He claimed to have slept with hundreds over the course of his short life. Steamo asked him, "What is the point?" His friend replied, "It's fun." Steamo thought for a second, and said "What you describe sounds more like a compulsion than a pleasure."

Steamo met a woman named Linda for sexual favors on a trip to Arizona. She disclosed to Steamo that she had surgery to remove her uterus. Steamo thought, "She only has the box it came in."

Steamo is not a fan of the razor. In fact, Steamo thinks that women that shave their pubic hair do so as an expression of their need to control their own bodies. A woman in her sixties showed Steamo her shaved 'who who ha ha'. Steamo realized this was her way to refuse to acknowledge her age. She was afraid of death.

Steamo likes to grant sexual favors to the grossly handicapped, both physically and mentally. Everyone deserves a good orgasm from a stranger now and then.

Steamo saw a young mother trying to control three small children while crossing the street. He commented to Soberanis, "I bet it was a lot more fun for her going in than coming out."

Chapter 8
Steamo's Advice on Peacefulness

Steamo likes to do yoga. He once met a snob who told him that yoga was meant to be done a certain way. Steamo chopped his head off with his claw, and returned to his practice.

Steamo has learned to watch his own mind and thoughts.

Steamo sometimes sits for hours in one place, unmoving. He is awake, but in a state of contemplation. Often times, people will walk right by him and think he is a statue. There is power and majesty in stillness.

Steamo says a good laugh and a long sleep are the two best cures for anything.

Steamo has three dogs and a cat. All of which he rescued from shelters. He tells all of his friends that pets are vital to health and happiness in life. Oftentimes even the most horrible psychological wounds can be healed through caring for an animal, and receiving its unconditional love.

After being around humans Steamo realized that people who live in the past live in regret while people who live in the future live in fear. Steamo lives in the present, enjoying every day to the fullest.

Steamo says "Don't stress them, NEXT them. Then pretend you never met them."

Steamo advises, "Live your life in peace—not pieces."